My dearest puppy, Storm,

I hope this letter reaches you safe
sound. You have been so brave
to fl_____ _____ Shadow.

Do not worry about me. I will hide here
until you are strong enough to return and
lead our pack. For now ___ ___ ust move on –
you must hide from S_____ ___ _____
If Shadow finds this ___
try to destroy it . . .

Find a good friend – someone to ___
my message to you. Because what I have to
say to you is important. What I have to say
is this: you must always

Please don't feel lonely. Trust in your friends
and all will be well.

Your loving mother,

Canista

Sue Bentley's books for children often include animals, fairies and wildlife. She lives in Northampton and enjoys reading, going to the cinema, relaxing by her garden pond and watching the birds feeding their babies on the lawn. At school she was always getting told off for daydreaming or staring out of the window – but she now realizes that she was storing up ideas for when she became a writer. She has met and owned many cats and dogs and each one has brought a special kind of magic to her life.

Sue Bentley

Magic Puppy

Twirling Tails

Illustrated by Angela Swan

PUFFIN

To Scarlet – sweet spotty girl with
the funny Dally grin

PUFFIN BOOKS

Published by the Penguin Group
Penguin Books Ltd, 80 Strand, London WC2R ORL, England
Penguin Group (USA) Inc., 375 Hudson Street, New York, New York 10014, USA
Penguin Group (Canada), 90 Eglinton Avenue East, Suite 700, Toronto, Ontario, Canada M4P 2Y3
(a division of Pearson Penguin Canada Inc.)
Penguin Ireland, 25 St Stephen's Green, Dublin 2, Ireland (a division of Penguin Books Ltd)
Penguin Group (Australia), 250 Camberwell Road, Camberwell, Victoria 3124, Australia
(a division of Pearson Australia Group Pty Ltd)
Penguin Books India Pvt Ltd, 11 Community Centre, Panchsheel Park, New Delhi – 110 017, India
Penguin Group (NZ), 67 Apollo Drive, Rosedale, North Shore 0632, New Zealand
(a division of Pearson New Zealand Ltd)
Penguin Books (South Africa) (Pty) Ltd, 24 Sturdee Avenue, Rosebank,
Johannesburg 2196, South Africa

Penguin Books Ltd, Registered Offices: 80 Strand, London WC2R ORL, England

puffinbooks.com

First published 2008
1

Text copyright © Sue Bentley, 2008
Illustrations copyright © Angela Swan, 2008
All rights reserved

The moral right of the author and illustrator has been asserted

Set in Bembo
Typeset by Palimpsest Book Production Limited,
Grangemouth, Stirlingshire
Made and printed in England by Clays Ltd, St Ives plc

British Library Cataloguing in Publication Data
A CIP catalogue record for this book is available from the British Library

ISBN: 978-0-141-32381-7

www.greenpenguin.co.uk

Penguin Books is committed to a sustainable future
for our business, our readers and our planet.
The book in your hands is made from paper
certified by the Forest Stewardship Council.

Prologue

As a terrifying howl rose into the
night air, the young silver-grey wolf
froze.

'Shadow!' Storm gasped. The evil lone
wolf who had attacked the Moon-claw
pack was very close.

Storm scanned the snow-covered
hillside with scared midnight-blue eyes.
He should have known it was

dangerous to come back home. He
needed to act quickly.

Sparks crackled in the young wolf's
thick fur and there was a flash of bright
gold light. Where Storm had stood,
there now crouched a tiny light-brown
puppy with a stocky body and shaggy
fur.

Storm's little puppy heart beat fast
as he leapt forward and ran across the
frozen ground. He hoped this disguise
would protect him until he found
somewhere to hide.

There were some snow-covered
bushes nearby. Storm wriggled under a
low branch and lay there trembling. A
rustling sound came from further back
in the bushes and icy snow fell on to
the tiny puppy. As the branches parted

to reveal the shape of a large wolf, Storm froze and his midnight-blue eyes widened in terror. Shadow had found him!

'I am glad to see you, my son. But it is not safe for you to be here,' the wolf rumbled softly.

'Mother!' Storm yipped in relief. His whole body wriggled and he wagged his sturdy little tail as he squirmed towards her.

Canista reached out one huge paw and gathered her disguised cub close. She whined fondly as she licked his little square muzzle and low-set ears, but her gold eyes filled with concern.

'You cannot stay. You are the only cub left in the Moon-claw pack. Shadow wants to be leader, but the others have scattered and will not follow him while you live.'

Storm growled softly and his midnight-blue eyes glowed with fury as he thought of the fierce wolf who had killed his father and three litter brothers.

'I am tired of hiding. I will fight Shadow now!' he yapped.

Canista shook her head slowly. 'Bravely said. But Shadow is too strong for you and I am still too weak from his poisoned bite to help you. Go back to the other world. Return when you are stronger and wiser and lead the Moon-claw pack.' As she stopped speaking, her gentle eyes clouded with pain.

Storm whined softly. He leaned close and huffed out a warm breath of shimmering gold sparks. They swirled round Canista's paw like golden smoke before disappearing into her grey fur.

Canista gave a long sigh. 'Thank you, Storm. The pain is lessening.'

But before Storm could finish healing her wound, another deafening howl rang out. The sound of mighty paws thudding on the frozen ground came closer.

'Shadow knows you are here! Go, now. Save yourself,' Canista urged.

Bright gold sparks bloomed in the tiny puppy's shaggy light-brown fur.

Storm whined softly as he felt the power building inside him. The glow of golden light around him grew brighter. And brighter . . .

Chapter
ONE

Kirsten Blake twirled her baton high into the air as she marched round the gym. She caught the baton perfectly without missing a beat of her routine.

'Yes,' she whispered to herself, delighted that all her practice was beginning to pay off.

Swinging her arms, Kirsten kept perfect time with the other Limelight

Majorettes as they wheeled and
interwove in time to the music.

'Shoulders back, heads up. Looking
good!' Molly the trainer cried. Her
blonde hair was tied back and she wore
shorts and a blue T-shirt with LM in
glittery letters on the front.

As the music ended, all the

majorettes stopped at exactly the same moment.

'Well done, everyone,' Molly praised. 'Take a break now. After you get yourselves a drink, can we all gather together, please? I want to talk to you.'

Kirsten wiped her face on a towel and then went to get a drink from the machine.

Molly was already there. She leaned down to take a can from the chute.

'You've really improved lately, Kirsten,' she said, smiling.

Kirsten felt a glow of pride. 'Thanks. I love baton twirling. I even march all round the house doing it. Dad says it's a wonder I'm not twirling in my sleep!'

Molly laughed. 'That would be one

way to get more practice in. But I can't say I recommend it!'

The gym door opened and a girl wearing jeans and a fleece sauntered in carrying a sports bag. She went over to a corner and dumped her bag.

It was Tracy Owen, Kirsten's best friend.

Kirsten and Tracy were in the same class at school and usually walked to majorette practice together. But this evening, Tracy had told Kirsten that she'd meet her there.

Kirsten noticed Molly looking across at Tracy. The trainer was shaking her head with annoyance.

Kirsten quickly got a second can from the machine and hurried straight over to Tracy. 'Here you are. I got you this.

Molly's on the warpath about you being late,' she warned her. 'Where've you been, anyway?'

'Thanks.' Tracy took the drink and popped the ring pull. 'Nowhere much,' she said in answer to Kirsten's question. 'I don't know why Molly's in such a stress. There's not exactly much going on here.'

'That's only because we're having a break, you muppet,' Kirsten said, giving her a friendly dig. 'We've all been practising like maniacs. You should have seen me. I just did the most mega-high twirl *and* I managed to catch the baton!'

'Good for you,' Tracy murmured without enthusiasm.

Kirsten's high spirits wavered a bit.

Tracy seemed in a strange mood. She saw that Molly was coming over.

'Hello, Tracy,' Molly said. 'I expected you to come straight over to me. Haven't you got something you want to say?'

Tracy flushed. 'Um . . . I s'pose so. Sorry I'm a bit late.'

'You're over an hour late! And it's not

the first time. I think you owe me an explanation,' Molly said.

Tracy shuffled her feet and looked at the floor. 'I popped in to see one of my classmates. She's . . . er . . . really poorly. We got talking and I didn't notice the time.'

Kirsten was puzzled. Why hadn't Tracy told *her* that? And she couldn't think of any girls in their class who were off sick. She threw Tracy a questioning look, but her friend didn't meet her eye.

Molly sighed. 'We'll say no more about it. But will you make sure that you get here on time from now on?'

Tracy nodded.

'Good. Finish getting changed and then come and sit with the others. I'm about to make an announcement,'

Molly said as she walked away.

'She's dead bossy,' Tracy grumbled, pulling on her trainers. 'I'm fed up of her ordering us all around like we're little kids.'

'Well, she is the trainer. That's what they do,' Kirsten said reasonably.

Tracy rolled her eyes. 'Yeah, well. She should lighten up. So I was late. It's not a crime, is it?' She stomped moodily over to a pile of gym mats.

Kirsten followed her and they sat down to listen to Molly, who was already speaking.

'. . . and as you know, the new shopping arcade in the High Street is almost finished. In two weeks' time, it's going to be officially opened by the mayor. There'll be street performers,

jugglers and a fair in the market square.
And we've been asked to lead the
Grand Parade. The Limelight Majorettes
will be marching along to the music of
a brass band!' Molly said with a flourish.

'Wow! That's cool!' Kirsten breathed,
as excited chatter broke out all around
her and even Tracy looked impressed.

It was Kirsten's dream to perform with the Limelight Majorettes, but only the A team marched in public and went in for competitions. She and Tracy were still in the B team.

Molly smiled round at all the eager faces. 'This is a great chance for us to show everyone what we can do. I want as many as possible of you to take part. So I'm going to move those of you who are ready into the A team.

'. . . Annie and Rosa. And Jacqui you'll all be moving up. And last but not least . . . Kirsten, you'll be joining the A team.'

'Me? Yay! That's fantastic!' Kirsten cried, delightedly bouncing up and down on the springy gym mats.

Tracy sat there with her arms folded, saying nothing.

Kirsten's high spirits took a dent as she realized that her friend's name hadn't been called out.

Molly clapped her hands. 'OK, everyone. Let's have another run-through.'

As the others dispersed, Kirsten stood up and then pulled Tracy to her feet.

'Molly. I think you've forgotten someone – Tracy!' she whispered urgently.

Molly shook her head. 'I didn't forget. I'm just not sure that Tracy wants to give one hundred per cent to the LMs right now. But I'd be happy to be proved wrong,' she said more gently, giving Tracy a meaningful look before she walked away.

Tracy watched her go without speaking.

Kirsten looked at her friend. 'Did you hear that? Molly more or less said that if you work really hard at practice now, you'll get into the A team too!' she said eagerly.

Tracy shrugged. 'Who cares? Maybe Helena's right. Dressing up like a chocolate soldier is pretty stupid –' She stopped suddenly. 'I'd better start work before Molly has a fit.' Tracy went to join some girls who were doing warm-ups.

Kirsten frowned. Did Tracy mean Helena Simpson, the new girl in class? Helena was popular with everyone and gave noisy opinions about everything. Kirsten didn't think Tracy even knew her that well.

A suspicion came over her. What if Tracy had just been at Helena's house? But that couldn't be right because Tracy said her classmate had been sick and Helena had been fine at school earlier. Unless Tracy was fibbing . . .

Kirsten didn't want to believe it. She wandered miserably into the toilets. There was no one else in there as she splashed her face at a basin. But as she looked back up into the mirrors, a dazzling flash of bright gold light lit up the whole room behind her.

'Oh!' Kirsten took a step backwards, rubbing at her eyes. When her sight cleared she turned to see a tiny puppy standing about a metre away on the tiled floor. It had light-brown shaggy fur, a little square muzzle and enormous midnight-blue eyes.

'I need to hide. Can you help me?' it woofed.

Chapter
TWO

Kirsten's jaw dropped and she stared at the puppy in total amazement. She must be more upset by the idea of Tracy and Helena meeting behind her back than she thought. She'd actually just imagined that the puppy had spoken to her!

'Hello. Aren't you a little cutie? Where did you just come from?' she crooned, bending down to talk to it.

She'd never seen a puppy with such bright blue eyes before.

The puppy pricked up its ears. It sat down and put its head on one side. 'I have come from far away. I am Storm of the Moon-claw pack. What is your name?'

'You really *can* talk!' Kirsten gasped, almost losing her balance and toppling backwards on to her behind. She just managed to grab hold of a nearby washbasin and steady herself before rising to her feet.

Kirsten felt like pinching herself to make sure she wasn't dreaming. Talking puppies didn't just appear out of thin air in gym washrooms. They only existed in fairy stories.

But Storm still sat there, looking up at her trustingly. The tiny puppy seemed to be waiting for her reply.

'I'm Kirsten. Kirsten Blake,' she found herself saying. 'I'm . . . er . . . one of the Limelight Majorettes. We practise here twice a week.'

Storm dipped his head in a formal little bow. 'I am honoured to meet you, Kirsten.'

'Um . . . me too,' Kirsten said. Her curiosity was starting to get the better of her shock. Despite its tiny size, the cute puppy didn't seem to be too scared of her.

'What was that you said about a . . . Moon-something?' she asked him.

Storm lifted his little head proudly.
'The Moon-claw pack. My mother and
father were the leaders. But Shadow, an
evil lone wolf, attacked us. Now my
father and litter brothers are dead and my
mother is wounded. Shadow wants to be
leader now, but the other wolves will not
follow him. They are waiting for me.'

Kirsten frowned as she took this in.
'But how can you lead a wolf pack?
You're just a tiny pu—'

'Please, stand back,' Storm ordered.

He stood up. Bright gold sparks
bloomed in his shaggy light-brown fur
and there was another dazzling flash of
light.

Kirsten blinked hard as the light
gradually faded. The tiny puppy had
gone and in its place there stood a

majestic young silver-grey wolf with glowing midnight-blue eyes. Its thick neck-ruff shimmered, as if it had been sprinkled all over with gold dust.

'Storm?' As Kirsten eyed the wolf's strong muscles, powerful oversized paws and long sharp teeth, she started to back away.

'Yes, it is me, Kirsten. Do not be afraid. I will not harm you,' Storm said in a deep velvety growl.

Kirsten hardly had time to get used to seeing Storm as his amazing real self before there was a final burst of bright light and a fountain of gold sparks sprinkled down around her and fizzed out as they hit the floor tiles. Storm stood there once again as a tiny helpless puppy.

'Wow!' she breathed in wonder. 'That was incredible. No one would know that you're really a wolf in disguise.'

'Shadow will know if he finds me,' Storm woofed nervously. 'Can you help me? I need to find somewhere safe to hide.'

Kirsten could see that the puppy was beginning to tremble all over. She felt her heart melt. As his real self, Storm was stunning, but as a cute dewy-eyed

little puppy he was the most adorable thing Kirsten had ever seen.

She bent down and picked him up. As she stroked the fur on Storm's deep little chest, he reached up and licked her. His whiskery little muzzle brushed her chin.

'That really tickles!' Kirsten said, giggling and pulling back out of reach. 'I've decided that you're coming home with me. Mum and Dad won't mind. We belong to Paws, an animal charity, and we're always looking after cats and dogs until they can be re-homed.'

'I would like to live with you very much!' Storm yapped eagerly. His little mouth opened in a doggy grin, revealing his sharp white teeth.

'I can't wait to show you to Tracy,'

Kirsten said, hoping that maybe this news would shake Tracy out of her odd mood and then their friendship could get back to normal. 'She's my best friend. She's going to be so –' Kirsten began.

'No, Kirsten!' Storm reared up to look into her face, his sparkling blue eyes suddenly serious. 'I am sorry, but you cannot tell anyone about me. Promise me that you will keep my secret.'

Kirsten felt disappointed that she couldn't tell her friend the exciting news about Storm, but if it meant keeping Storm safe she decided she wouldn't say anything. Besides, Tracy didn't seem to be in the mood for sharing secrets right now.

'OK, I promise. Cross my heart,' she said.

As Storm relaxed against her again, Kirsten had a sudden thought. 'There're loads of people in the gym. How am I going to smuggle you out of here without anyone noticing?'

Storm's teeth showed in another doggy grin. 'Do not worry. I will use my magic, so that only you will be able to see and hear me.'

'You can make yourself invisible? That's *so* cool!' Kirsten said. 'Maybe you'd better do it now, before someone else comes in here.'

Storm's midnight-blue eyes glinted and a few tiny sparks flared in his light-brown fur. 'It is done.'

'Really? Wow! Well, I'd better get

back to practice now. Let's go.' Kirsten
put Storm down on to the tiled floor
and he trotted at her heels as she went
to rejoin the others.

Kirsten felt quite tense. Even though
Storm had told her that he was
invisible, she couldn't quite make herself
believe it and kept expecting someone
to notice him. But when no one did,

Kirsten relaxed and took her place in line.

As she began twirling her baton, Kirsten's heart lifted at the thought of the magical little friend who was sitting watching and her worries about whether Helena was trying to get friendly with Tracy faded for the time being.

Chapter
THREE

'What an absolutely gorgeous puppy!'
Kirsten's mum said. She bent down to
stroke the tiny puppy's low-set ears. 'I
think he's a Border terrier. Fancy you
just finding him wandering down the
main road all by himself like that.'

'Mmm. Weird, wasn't it?' Kirsten said
vaguely.

'What did Tracy say? Didn't she want

to take Storm home with her?' her mum asked.

'I didn't walk home with Tracy. She rushed off the minute practice ended. I expect she had to meet her mum from work or something,' Kirsten told her.

Mrs Blake raised her eyebrows, but didn't comment.

'Anyway, Storm's one lucky pup to have found us, isn't he? He told me that he –' Kirsten stopped quickly as she realized that she would have to be a lot more careful about keeping Storm's secret. 'I . . . um . . . mean, he obviously needed a home. And I thought he could stay with us,' she finished hurriedly.

'Well, we're certainly used to looking after strays.' Her mum smiled and bent

down to pick Storm up. The little
puppy whined and began licking her all
over her face.

Mrs Blake laughed. 'Thanks, Storm,
but I've had a wash today! I like his
name. It really suits him,' she said to her
daughter. 'I'll phone Paws and let them
know that we've got a puppy that needs

a permanent home. We'd better put a note in the newsagent's window too, just in case an owner's looking for him.'

'Good idea,' Kirsten agreed, feeling confident that no one was going to be claiming this particular puppy. 'And if no one comes for Storm, we could keep him forever, couldn't we?' she said in her best pleading voice.

Her mum frowned. 'You know the rules, love. We look after animals until they can be re-homed. If we kept every stray we'd be overrun with cats and dogs.'

'OK,' Kirsten sighed, knowing that she'd have to be satisfied with that for now, but she secretly promised herself to work hard to change her mum's mind. 'I'll take Storm into the kitchen

35

and get him some food. I bet he's really
hungry.'

'Food?' Storm barked eagerly, his ears
twitching. He started squirming to be
let down.

Mrs Blake smiled as she placed the
wriggling little puppy back on the floor.
'I could swear he understood every
word you just said!'

Kirsten bit back a grin as she went
out with Storm ambling after her. 'If
only Mum knew how right she was!'
she whispered to him.

In the kitchen, Kirsten forked tinned
dog food into a bowl and stood
watching as Storm bolted it down in
about half a minute.

'Thank you. That was delicious,' he
woofed, licking his chops clean.

After she'd washed his bowl, Kirsten let Storm out for a short run in the garden and then got herself a drink and some biscuits.

'Let's go to my room and I'll show you where you can sleep,' she said, heading towards the stairs. On the way, Kirsten popped her head round the sitting-room door and spoke to her mum and dad. 'I'm going to finish my art homework and then get ready for bed. See you later.'

'All right, sweetheart,' her dad said.

In her bedroom, Kirsten spread an old blanket on her duvet and then lifted Storm on to it. 'There you are. A cosy bed, especially for you.'

With an eager little whine, Storm began nosing about and scrabbling the blanket into messy folds. Once he was satisfied, he plonked down and rested his button-like black nose on his front paws.

'This is a good place. I feel safe here,' he yawned.

'Glad you like it,' Kirsten said. She smiled at the sleepy puppy, feeling a surge of affection for him. She took a folder and pencil case from her school bag. 'We're studying Van Gogh in art. I'm making a copy of his painting of sunflowers with felt-tips . . .'

But Storm wasn't listening. He sighed contentedly and moments later, tiny snores rose from his curled little form.

The following morning, Kirsten was almost ready to leave for school. She

felt a bit nervous about seeing Tracy.
This new friendship with Helena was
playing on her mind and she wondered
whether she should mention her
worries or just say nothing.

Kirsten sighed as she packed her
folder and the finished sunflower
picture into her shoulder bag. Storm sat
on the front-door mat watching her as
she reached for her coat.

'I hope you won't be too bored while

I'm away,' Kirsten said as she fastened
the buttons. 'I'll take you for a lovely
long walk as soon as I get back –
promise!' she said, smiling at him.

Storm jumped up and wagged his
sturdy little tail. 'We can go for a walk
right now. I will come with you,' he
woofed eagerly.

'I really wish you could, but we're

not allowed to bring pets to school,' Kirsten explained regretfully.

'But I am not a pet!' Storm yapped. 'And no one will know that I am there.'

Kirsten remembered that Storm could make himself invisible, but she was still unsure about having a lively puppy in the classroom. It could lead to all kinds of complications.

'Well . . . OK, then. But you'll have to be extra careful to stay out of everyone's way,' she decided. 'Our teacher Miss Strong is really nice, but she's quite strict.'

Storm's eyes sparkled with triumph. He turned and began pawing the front door impatiently.

Kirsten laughed at his cheekiness.

'Hey! Hang on, you! I think you should get in my shoulder bag. We have to cross some busy roads.'

'Very well,' Storm yapped. As soon as Kirsten opened her bag he scrambled inside.

Kirsten said goodbye to her mum before they set off for Chaucer Crescent, where Tracy lived.

'Tracy's house is number thirty-seven,' Kirsten told Storm as they walked along the pavement bordering an area of grass. 'I usually call for her. There she is now.'

Tracy was just coming out of her house. A tall girl with long blonde hair and a thin face was with her.

Kirsten recognized Helena Simpson. She stopped in dismay as her suspicions seemed to be confirmed. 'Why's she calling for Tracy? Everyone knows that Tracy's *my* best friend!'

Chapter
FOUR

Kirsten and Storm waited for the two girls to reach them. 'Hi, Tracy. Hi, Helena,' Kirsten said, trying to sound a lot more cheerful than she felt.

'Hi, Kirsten,' Helena replied.

'Helena's only just arrived. She thought we could all walk to school together,' Tracy said.

Kirsten shrugged. 'OK.'

'How did it go at majorettes' practice last night? Did you do loads of prancing about on tippy-toes?' Helena asked, smirking.

Kirsten was taken aback and took a moment to reply. 'That's ballet. We do marching routines with twirling batons and stuff. It's a bit like American cheerleaders.'

'Sounds OK. If you're about six years old!' Helena said, rolling her eyes as if she'd just made a clever joke.

Kirsten didn't laugh. 'You can be any age from five upwards. Some of the seniors are eighteen. I like being a majorette. It's fun.'

'You like showing off, you mean!' Helena crowed.

'No, I don't!' Kirsten felt her jaw drop.

'Kirsten's not like that,' Tracy defended her.

'Whatever,' Helena drawled. 'Anyway, last night I thought you said that baton twirling and marching were pathetic.'

Tracy looked uncomfortable. 'You said that. I only agreed with you because I thought you were joking!'

46

'You were with Helena last night?' Kirsten said to Tracy, trying to sound casual.

Her friend nodded. 'I went to help Helena with her homework. I was going to tell you. But after Molly had a go at me for being late for practice, I didn't get round to it. You don't mind, do you?'

Kirsten did mind, but she didn't want to show it. She made herself shrug. 'Course not. Why should I?'

Tracy looked relieved. She smiled at Helena. 'I told you Kirsten would be fine about it.'

'Oh good,' Helena said, smiling sweetly. 'Then we can all be best friends, can't we?'

No we can't, Kirsten wanted to shout. She and Tracy had been best friends since forever. They didn't need anyone else.

As they all made their way to school, Kirsten slipped her hand into her shoulder bag and gently stroked Storm's fuzzy little head, trying to ignore the horrible sinking feeling in her tummy. She was really glad that her new little friend would be with her all day.

Kirsten sat staring into space, gloomily threading her fingers. She was at her usual desk behind Tracy, near the back of the class. Helena sat a couple of desks away from them both, nearer to the front.

Storm was off somewhere, snuffling around and exploring the classroom, invisible to everyone except Kirsten.

Miss Strong the class teacher took the register. She was small and very pretty, with stylish hair. She had lots of pairs of designer glasses. Today she wore narrow purple ones.

'Here, Miss,' Kirsten answered when her name was called out.

As Miss Strong put the register away in her desk drawer, Kirsten caught sight of Storm.

The tiny puppy was just backing out of an open cupboard that he'd been investigating. Storm saw Kirsten looking at him. He gave an excited little woof and almost fell over his own paws as he came gambolling towards her.

Storm plonked himself down at her feet, his pink tongue lolling out. Despite herself, Kirsten couldn't help smiling. 'Having fun?' she whispered.

Storm nodded happily. 'There are many wonderful smells in here.'

Miss Strong's voice rang out again, almost making Kirsten jump.

'Right, class. Can you get your art folders out, please?'

Kirsten fished her folder out of her bag. As she spread the contents on to her desk, Storm leapt up to sit beside her. His light-brown fur was trailing tiny glimmering sparks.

Storm leaned forward curiously to see what Kirsten was doing. After quickly checking that no one was looking, she reached out to stroke him.

'I'm so glad that you're my friend,' she whispered.

'Me too,' Storm woofed softly.

As Kirsten sat back in her chair, something stung her below one eye. 'Ow!' she cried in surprise as a tightly rolled paper pellet bounced down on to her desk.

Helena waggled her ruler in the air, grinning triumphantly.

'That really hurt. It nearly hit me in the eye!' Kirsten fumed.

Helena rolled her eyes. '*Some* people can't take a joke,' she said under her breath.

Miss Strong looked up at them over the top of her glasses. 'Kirsten? Helena? What's going on?' she demanded.

'Nothing, Miss,' Kirsten said quickly,

but the teacher had already noticed the ruler in Helena's hand. 'Are you flicking things about, Helena? This isn't Reception class, for goodness' sake. Do I have to ask you to come and sit at the front so I can keep an eye on you?'

'No way, Miss,' Helena said, slapping the ruler on to her desk.

Miss Strong gave her a level look. 'I'm very glad to hear it. Now, get on with your work, please.'

Helena banged about, setting out brushes and paints. She then rose and swept to the back of the class to fill a jam jar at the sink.

'Thanks for nothing!' she hissed as she passed Kirsten.

'What? I didn't do anything!'

'You deliberately yelled out, so Miss

Strong saw me flicking pellets! I bet you just loved getting me into trouble,' Helena accused.

Kirsten didn't reply. She was too upset to notice Storm's furry brow dipping in a frown.

Helena turned the tap and filled the jam jar to the brim. As she sauntered back past Kirsten's desk, Helena pretended to trip. Her arm shot out as she 'accidentally' chucked water all over Kirsten's sunflower picture.

'Oops. Clumsy me!'

Kirsten gasped. 'Oh no! My painting. It's ruined!'

Helena smirked. 'Aw! Diddums!'

'You did that on purpose!' Kirsten cried, jumping to her feet.

Suddenly, she felt a strange prickling

sensation flow down her spine as huge golden sparks ignited in Storm's shaggy light-brown fur and his low-set ears crackled and fizzed with magical power.

Something very strange was about to happen.

Chapter
FIVE

Storm's bright midnight-blue eyes glowed as he lifted a tiny light-brown front paw and aimed a big *whoosh* of swirling glitter at Kirsten's flooded desk.

Kirsten watched in complete astonishment as the magical glitter flashed about, hoovering up the spilled water. Water droplets began rising upwards from her picture, like rain

falling in reverse. In seconds her picture
was as good as new.

All the water now formed a giant
shining teardrop. Storm waved his paw
again and, just as if someone had
pressed fast forward, the water shot
sideways and whizzed towards Helena,
who had now turned her back.

But Storm's aim was slightly off. The

giant teardrop missed Helena by a millimetre. *Splosh!* It smacked straight into Tracy and burst, drenching the front of her school jumper.

Tracy screeched in shock and leapt to her feet. 'What did you do that for?'

'It wasn't me . . . I mean . . . er . . . it was an accident,' Kirsten stammered. She could hardly explain that her invisible puppy friend was the culprit. Even if she had, Tracy wouldn't have believed her. 'Um . . . Sorry,' she finished lamely.

Helena grabbed a handful of paper towels and started mopping at Tracy's jumper. 'Kirsten just did that on purpose. She's jealous because you want to be friends with me and not only with her!'

'I am not!' Kirsten fumed. Even if she did feel a bit hurt, she certainly wouldn't have taken it out on Helena. 'Tracy can be friends with who she likes!'

'Tracy knows that. It's not like she needs *your* permission!' Helena shot back at her.

'That's quite enough!' Miss Strong stood there with her hands on her hips. 'What's got into you three today? You're like wild animals! Tracy, go into the cloakroom and get changed. Helena, go back to your seat. And Kirsten, get on with your work.'

'But, Miss . . .' Helena began.

'Now, if you please,' Miss Strong said firmly.

Helena slunk off and sat down, while Tracy went towards the cloakroom.

Kirsten stood there for a moment longer, still amazed by how quickly the argument had broken out. She was tempted to tell the teacher that Helena had started it. But she'd never been a snitch and she wasn't about to start being one now, however infuriating Helena was.

As Kirsten slowly sank on to her chair, Storm climbed into her lap. 'I am

sorry. I seem to have made things worse for you,' he whined softly.

'That's all right. You were just trying to help,' Kirsten whispered.

She was dying to give Storm a big cuddle to show that she wasn't cross with him, but she daren't risk it with Helena still glaring at her across the room. She had to settle for just patting him.

'I'm going to the squash club. Do you want a lift to the gym?' Mr Blake asked, after Kirsten had helped clear away after supper that evening.

'That would be great,' Kirsten said.

She thought about phoning Tracy and asking if she wanted picking up. But Tracy hadn't spoken to her since the

soaking incident in the art class. Kirsten
decided that it might be better to wait
and try to talk to her during practice.
Clearing the air between them might
be easier without Helena around.

Kirsten sat in the back of the car
with Storm on her lap as her dad drove
to the gym. 'You won't have to be
invisible at the gym,' Kirsten whispered.
'I'm sure Molly won't mind me
bringing you, as long as she sees that
you're really well behaved.'

Storm nodded.

As the car drew up, Kirsten got out
with Storm in her arms. 'Thanks for
the lift. See you later, Dad,' she said,
waving as he drove off.

Kirsten and Storm went inside with
some other girls who had just arrived.

They all crowded round and wanted to know about Storm. Molly was getting changed into some tracksuit bottoms. She looked up as Kirsten, Storm and the other girls came into the changing room.

'What's all the commotion? Oh, what an adorable puppy,' Molly said as a big smile spread across her face. 'What's his name?'

'Storm,' Kirsten told her. 'I haven't had him long, but I love him to bits.'

'Who wouldn't love him?' said one of the girls stroking Storm. 'He's so cute!'

'Enough of the fussing already! Off you all go and get changed,' Molly said. She looked thoughtful. 'It's about time the Limelight Majorettes had a mascot. A puppy like Storm would be perfect.

But he'd have to be well trained. I
suppose Storm is too young, Kirsten?'

'No, no! Storm could do it,' Kirsten
exclaimed. 'I've . . . er . . . been
encouraging him to march with me
when I practise baton twirling at
home.'

'Well, if that's so, I'd love to see him

doing it. Do you think you can show us before practice starts? We're still waiting for a few girls to arrive,' Molly said.

'Um . . . Right now?' Kirsten said. She hadn't banked on an instant demonstration and started to regret her impulsive outburst. 'I'll just ask St– I mean, I'll just get Storm ready. He . . . er . . . has to get into the mood.'

'Fine,' Molly said. 'Come on, everyone. Let's leave Kirsten and Storm to it.' She ushered the other girls out of the changing room.

The moment they were alone, Kirsten sank on to a bench. 'Oh heck. Now what am I going to do? I'm sorry, Storm. I should have asked if you wanted to be our mascot. We can forget the whole idea. I'll think up some excuse to tell Molly.'

'Wait, Kirsten,' Storm yapped, his large midnight-blue eyes glinting. 'What would I have to do?'

'Well, you'd have to wear a little uniform in the troupe's colours and walk beside me as I march in the parade. Mascots are supposed to bring good luck,' Kirsten explained.

Storm showed his sharp little teeth in a grin. 'That sounds good. I would like to try!'

'You would? That's brilliant!' Kirsten said delightedly. She quickly pulled on her T-shirt and short pleated skirt. 'Now we have to convince Molly that you're the right puppy for the job. I'll talk you through the routine as I do it. OK?'

As Kirsten returned to the gym with
Storm, she could feel her palms
sweating. Despite the little puppy's
eagerness, she was really nervous about
messing up in front of everyone.

The door opened as more girls
arrived for practice. Kirsten saw Tracy
come in. Helena was just behind her.

Kirsten groaned inwardly. That's all
she needed.

'Quiet, please, everyone,' Molly called out. 'Ready, Kirsten?' she said, slotting a CD into the player.

Kirsten felt her face growing hot, but she forced herself to concentrate. She struck a pose and smiled encouragingly at Storm. He was looking up at her with his ears pricked, awaiting instructions.

As the intro music rang out, Kirsten began the routine. 'Right, forward, left wheel. Follow me . . .' she instructed Storm.

Storm lifted his chin, picked up his paws and marched confidently beside her.

Kirsten's baton flashed as she twirled it expertly, while high-stepping in time to the music. Storm followed her every

word and wheeled back and forth as
she did the complicated routine.

As the music faded Kirsten stopped.
Beside her, Storm stretched out one
front paw and dipped his head in a
bow.

A chorus of cheers rang out, followed
by a burst of applause. Kirsten was
shocked to see that even Tracy and
Helena were clapping enthusiastically.

Molly came over to congratulate her.
'You were right, Kirsten. Storm will be
a wonderful mascot for us. We'll have to
see about getting him a uniform. Do
you think you'll be able to bring him
to practice regularly, so that he can get
used to marching with the whole
troupe?'

Kirsten glanced across at Storm, who

was rolling on his back so that he could have his tummy rubbed by two majorettes. 'I think I might have a job actually keeping him away!'

Chapter
SIX

As Tracy came over, Kirsten steeled herself to apologize again for soaking her in class earlier.

But her friend seemed to have forgotten all about it. She bent down to stroke Storm. 'Hello, boy. Aren't you lovely?' She looked up at Kirsten. 'Is he one of the strays your mum and dad are always trying to find homes for?'

Kirsten nodded, and spotted Helena wandering over to join them. 'He's a new one. Storm's a really special little pup.' She smiled secretly to herself, imagining the look on Tracy's face if she could have known how special Storm *really* was. 'I'm hoping Mum will let me keep him. I'm waiting for the right time to ask her.'

'I wouldn't mind having a new puppy,' Helena said wistfully. 'But my mum doesn't like pets. She says they're messy and looking after them takes up too much time.'

'That's a shame,' Kirsten said. 'I couldn't imagine not having a pet.'

'You're really lucky to be able to look after all kinds of different puppies,' Helena went on. 'What sort is Storm? Is he a mongrel?'

Kirsten smiled. 'No. But I wouldn't mind if he was. He's a Border terrier.'

'I've never heard of those,' Helena said, looking interested. 'Are they rare?'

'I'm not sure. You'd have to ask my mum. She's the expert,' Kirsten said. *Helena seems to like puppies almost as much as I do*, she thought with surprise.

Helena bent down to stroke Storm. 'Hello, little fella!'

At first Storm eyed Helena warily but then he allowed her to pat him and began slowly wagging his tail. Kirsten noticed that Storm seemed to be slightly warming towards Helena.

'I guess we really should do some work,' Kirsten said eventually to Tracy as Helena stood up again.

Tracy nodded. 'Will you be OK by yourself, Helena?'

'I'll be fine watching. Can I look after Storm, if he's not practising with you all the time?' Helena said.

Kirsten was about to say that Storm didn't need looking after, but when she glanced at him he gave a small woof of agreement.

'Sure. Why not,' Kirsten said generously. Storm was with her all day. It wouldn't hurt for Helena to share him for a few minutes.

The rest of practice went well. Tracy worked hard, earning herself some praise from Molly, and Storm followed all the routines perfectly. Kirsten noticed that Helena was sitting watching everything closely. She was unusually quiet.

Mr Blake called in just as practice ended. He was passing the gym anyway and wondered if Kirsten and Storm wanted a lift home.

'Can we take Tracy and Helena too?' Kirsten asked, deciding to try not to be so suspicious of Helena all the time.

They all piled into the car. Helena sat

on the back seat with Tracy. 'I didn't know being a majorette was so complicated. You have to do millions of warm-ups and stretches and leg-strengthening stuff. It's like you're real athletes.'

Kirsten glanced at her in the wing mirror. 'We are! You have to be really fit to do the routines.'

'Dad's always telling me I should do

some sports. I think I might ask Molly about joining,' Helena mused.

Kirsten raised her eyebrows. She was starting not to mind Helena so much. But she still wasn't sure if she liked the idea of her joining in with everything that she and Tracy did together. She decided not to say anything just now.

When Mr Blake stopped outside Tracy's house, Tracy and Helena both got out.

'Thanks for the lift,' they chorused. 'See you in the morning,' Tracy called.

'Bye!' Kirsten waved.

Once they got home, Kirsten asked her mum and dad if they'd like some hot chocolate. She spooned chocolate powder into three mugs. While she was waiting for the kettle to boil, she rummaged in a cupboard and found a tasty bone-shaped dog chew for Storm.

'Here you go. You deserve a yummy treat. I was so proud of you at practice,' she told him.

'I enjoyed being a mascot,' Storm yapped.

He bounced forward on to his short front legs and grabbed the chew. Picking it up, he trotted around the kitchen with both ends of it sticking out of his mouth.

Kirsten made the drinks and put them on a tray. She laughed as Storm followed her into the sitting room with his prize. 'You'd better sit on your old blanket to eat that or Mum'll go spare!' she whispered.

★

Kirsten jogged across the school playing field a few mornings later with Storm gambolling along invisibly beside her.

Miss Strong was already on the hockey pitch handing out yellow and green sashes and organizing the class into teams. Kirsten was in the Greens and Tracy and Helena were in the Yellows.

'Kirsten and Tracy, you're centre forwards, so you'll bully off.' Miss Strong looked around, checking that everyone was in position.

Kirsten flexed her knees as she faced Tracy on the centre line.

Storm began leaping around her ankles excitedly. 'Tell me what to do and I will follow you, Kirsten!' he yapped so that only Kirsten heard him.

With a tingle of alarm, it dawned on
Kirsten that Storm thought playing
hockey was like a majorette routine. He
didn't realize that he could be kicked
by a player or hit by a hockey stick.
She couldn't warn him of the danger
with everyone so close.

Miss Strong picked up the whistle
dangling by a cord round her neck.

Phee-eep! The game was on.

Kirsten won the bully off. She hared down the field, hoping to get away from the other players. Once she was out of earshot, she'd be able to tell Storm to get off the pitch.

Storm gave a joyful bark and dashed after Kirsten, his strong little legs eating up the grass. Kirsten glanced sideways at him as she ran with the ball, but Helena was pounding after her and she still couldn't warn Storm of the danger.

'To me, Kirsten!' one of the players cried.

'Come on, Yellows. Tackle her!'

Helena dodged forward. She tackled Kirsten and won the ball. Lifting her stick, Helena swivelled, about to send the ball out to a winger.

Kirsten gasped with horror as Storm dashed forward and stood in front of Helena. He was right in the path of the rock-hard hockey ball.

Chapter
SEVEN

'Look out!' Quick as a flash, Kirsten dropped her stick and shoved against Helena with her whole body.

'Oh!' Helena skidded and only just managed to stop herself from falling over. Her hockey stick slammed down, missing the ball.

Pheep! Miss Strong blew the whistle for a foul as she ran towards them. 'I

saw that, Kirsten! You did it deliberately.
I will not tolerate this behaviour. Go
and get changed and wait for me in the
classroom.'

Helena stood there with a hurt
expression on her face. She looked
more upset than angry.

Kirsten felt terrible, but at least Storm

was uninjured. Her shoulders drooped as she trailed across the pitch.

Tracy jogged up to her. 'What happened? I thought you were starting to like Helena.'

'I was . . . I am . . .' Kirsten said.

'Well, you've got a funny way of showing it!'

'I wasn't *trying* to hurt Helena, honest!' Kirsten protested. 'But I couldn't help it –' She stopped. There was nothing else she could say without giving away Storm's secret. 'I can't explain. But you have to believe me.'

Tracy looked puzzled. 'I don't know, Kirsten . . .'

Sighing heavily, Kirsten left the pitch and headed for the changing rooms.

Storm bounded after her. 'Thank you

for saving me, Kirsten,' he panted. 'But now you are in even more trouble because of me.'

'I'll live with it,' Kirsten said resignedly. 'It's more important that you're OK. It was my fault, anyway. I should have warned you to stay off the hockey pitch. Don't worry, Miss Strong will probably make me write out a hundred lines or tidy the art cupboard. It's no big deal.'

But the teacher decided on a more serious punishment.

'Detention!' Kirsten cried, gaping at her. 'But I *can't* stay behind after school, Miss. I've got majorette practice.'

'I'm afraid you should have thought of that earlier,' Miss Strong said firmly, adjusting her glasses — today they were

bright red. 'I'll let your parents know
that you'll be late home.'

At the end of the day's lessons,
Kirsten sat with her chin propped in
her hands as everyone filed out of class.

'Hard luck,' Helena said as she passed
Kirsten's desk. 'No hard feelings, eh?'
And for once, she sounded as if she
meant it.

'Thanks,' Kirsten said, managing a half-smile. Helena was being really fair about this and Kirsten realized that she'd stopped minding so much about Helena becoming best friends with her and Tracy. Maybe it could work – if *she* hadn't now messed things up.

Miss Strong picked up a pile of papers from her desk. 'I've a few things to do in the staffroom. I won't be long. Carry on with your art project, please.' She went out and closed the classroom door behind her.

Kirsten groaned. 'Now what am I going to do? I can't afford to miss practice. There're only a few left before the town parade.'

Storm's furry face lit up. 'I have an idea!'

Kirsten felt a familiar prickling sensation down her spine as bright gold sparks danced in Storm's shaggy light-brown fur and his bristly whiskers glowed with electricity.

There was a bright flash and a silent explosion of sparks. Pop! Kirsten's CD player appeared out of thin air and floated on to the floor. *Crack!* Her baton clattered down beside the CD player. *Rustle!* Her school uniform was magically transformed into a T-shirt, a short pleated skirt and trainers.

Kirsten beamed at her tiny friend. 'Thanks, Storm. You're a star!'

She switched on the CD player at a low volume so no one would overhear, and the intro music softly started. For the next twenty minutes or so, Kirsten and Storm marched up and down and round the empty classroom. The tiny puppy knew the routine now and Kirsten hardly needed to tell him what to do.

'That was great,' Kirsten puffed, flexing her fingers after all the baton twirling. 'I can't wait until we're marching in the real parade! Let's do

one more run-through before Miss
Strong comes back.'

Storm suddenly froze and his ears
twitched. 'I think she is coming now!'

Waving a paw he sent another spray
of golden sparks through the air.
Crackle! The CD player and baton
disappeared instantly and Kirsten was,
once again, wearing her school uniform.

As the classroom door began to
open, Kirsten realized that she was
nowhere near her desk where she was
supposed to be working on her

project. 'Uh-oh, Miss Strong's going to go bananas. I'll probably get triple detention now!'

There was a sudden mega-*whoosh* of movement and Kirsten felt herself flying through the air.

'Oof!' She landed in her chair with a bump.

She was only just in time. Miss Strong's small neat figure appeared in the doorway.

'You can clear away your things and go now, Kirsten. I think I've made my point. Let's have no more of this silly behaviour. It's just not like you.'

'No, Miss. Thanks,' Kirsten said in a subdued voice.

Storm had a mischievous look on his face. He had obviously really enjoyed their practice session and was disappointed that it had been cut short. Leaping up to balance on his back legs, he began pirouetting towards the door.

A big bubble of laughter threatened to burst from Kirsten's lips. She stuffed her work into her school bag and fled into the corridor.

Chapter
EIGHT

Luckily Kirsten's mum and dad weren't too annoyed with her for getting detention and accepted her explanation that it was all a mistake.

'You haven't got a mean bone in your body, Kirsten Blake,' her dad said. 'Even if you do have a one-track mind about being in the majorettes!'

'Me?' Kirsten made her eyes all big.

'I don't know what you mean,' she joked.

They all laughed as they settled down to supper.

Kirsten's mum spotted Storm sitting beside Kirsten's chair. She shook her head. 'You know I can never find that puppy when you're at school. He doesn't come out of hiding, however much I call him or waft a dish of food about. But it's amazing how he always appears the second you come home.'

'Amazing,' Kirsten echoed innocently, around a mouthful of macaroni cheese.

A couple of evenings later, Molly phoned. She wanted Storm's measurements for his costume. Kirsten said she'd get them and then ring her back.

As soon as she'd hung up, Kirsten searched out her mum's tape measure. She lifted Storm up on to a table and then looped the tape round his compact little body.

Storm wagged his tail and tried to twist round to lick her face.

'Hey! Stop wriggling! This is like a juggling act!' Kirsten was struggling to hold the ends of the tape together with one hand while jotting figures on to a piece of paper with the other.

Finally it was done. 'I'll give these measurements to Molly. I can't wait to see your costume!'

On the following Saturday afternoon, Kirsten decided to take Storm for a walk before meeting up with Tracy and Helena at a row of shops along the main road. A new fast food place called Smoothers had just opened. They had arranged to have a milkshake with their pocket money before going to practice.

'I don't mind about Helena joining the Limelight Majorettes,' Kirsten told Storm. 'I thought she'd just come along to mess about, but she seems serious about it. I heard Molly saying that she thinks Helena's going to be really good.'

'I am glad that you are good friends with Helena now,' Storm woofed.

We're almost there, Kirsten thought, a small smile on her face.

Kirsten said her goodbyes to her parents and then she and Storm set off.

They headed to a short alleyway that led to a field at the back of some houses. The fences of all the rear gardens backed on to the field.

Storm nosed about in the grass, seeking out interesting smells and then raced around enjoying himself. He found a muddy twig and held it in his little front paws to chew one end.

Suddenly, Kirsten heard loud growling and barking coming from behind one of the wooden fences. A noise like scrabbling claws filled the air as the unseen dogs tried to get into the field.

Storm yelped and dropped the twig. He rushed over to Kirsten and crouched beside her, trembling from head to foot.

'What's wrong? Have you hurt your mouth on that wood?' Kirsten said worriedly. She picked him up and cradled him in her arms.

Storm's midnight-blue eyes widened in terror. 'Shadow knows where I am. He has used his magic on those dogs. They are trying to get to me.'

Kirsten's heart missed a beat as she realized that her friend was in great danger. Her mind whirled as she tried to think of the best thing to do. 'That's a pretty high fence. I don't think they can get over,' she judged. 'But you'd better hide in my bag, just in case. We're leaving, right now!'

Kirsten opened her shoulder bag and tucked the terrified puppy inside. Storm immediately curled up into a tight ball and lay there shaking.

Her pulse racing, Kirsten jogged back

towards the alleyway. She clutched her bag tightly so that Storm wasn't jostled about too much.

'I hope we don't meet any more of Shadow's dogs. How will I be able to tell if they're dangerous?' Kirsten asked nervously.

'They will have cruel pale eyes and extra long teeth.' Storm's muffled woof rose from her bag.

Once she was back out on the street, Kirsten gradually slowed down. No fierce dogs had run after them and the growling and snarling grew faint and then stopped altogether.

'I think they've given up,' she puffed, feeling weak with relief.

Storm uncurled and gingerly peered out of the unzipped bag. He tensed as he listened hard and then his whole body relaxed. 'You are right, Kirsten. I am safe for the moment. But if Shadow finds me again I may have to leave suddenly, without saying goodbye.'

Kirsten experienced a sharp pang at the thought of losing her friend. She knew that she would never be ready to let him go. 'I hope that evil Shadow never finds you and then you can stay with me forever!'

Storm twisted to look up at her with serious midnight-blue eyes. 'I cannot do that. One day I must return to my own world to lead the Moon-claw pack.'

'I know,' Kirsten said in a small voice, but she didn't really want to think about it. She was determined to enjoy every single moment with her magical

friend. She tried changing the subject.
'I bet Tracy and Helena are already at
Smoothers. Let's go and meet them.'

Storm sat up and rested his front paws
outside the shoulder bag as Kirsten
turned on to the busy main road. A bit
further on, she saw Tracy and Helena on
the opposite side of the road. They were
just passing a video hire shop.

They spotted her too and waved.

Kirsten walked towards a pedestrian crossing in front of a building with scaffolding covering it. A clanging noise came from high up where builders were at work.

As Kirsten went to press the button to cross, there was a shout.

'Look out below!' someone warned.

Kirsten glanced behind her and looked up. A heavy bucket clanged on to one of the scaffolding boards and then came tumbling downwards. It was heading straight for her and Storm.

Kirsten froze. Her legs turned to water as she gathered herself for a painful collision.

But familiar bright sparks glittered in Storm's shaggy fur and a huge spray of gold sparks shot upwards. The bucket faltered as if Kirsten had pressed slow motion on a TV remote. A fine dusting of sparks drifted down to settle on Kirsten and weird rippling feelings ran up the ends of her fingers and toes and zipped through her body.

There was a sudden jolt as the bucket crashed down on top of her and Storm.

Kirsten gasped as it passed *right through* her. She felt a slurpy sensation, like a jelly wobbling and a sucking *plop!* as the heavy bucket clanged on to the pavement and bounced away harmlessly.

She heard running steps. Two builders emerged from inside the building, looking white-faced.

'Thank goodness. It just missed her!' one of them said shakily.

The other one picked up the bucket. He scratched his head. 'How the blazes . . . You sure you're all right, love?'

Kirsten quickly gathered her wits. 'I'm fine. No problem. Got to go!' As the green man flashed up on the crossing, Kirsten hurried across the road. 'Phew! That was close! Thanks, Storm,' she whispered.

'You are welcome,' Storm barked.

Helena and Tracy were hurrying along the pavement to meet them. 'What just happened? We heard shouting and a massive crash,' Tracy said.

'Was there an accident?' Helena asked worriedly.

'Nah! It was no big deal. Just two builders making lots of noise,' Kirsten said. Her face lit up with mischief. She dodged nimbly round Tracy and began sprinting towards the shops. 'Last one inside Smoothers pays for the milkshakes!'

'You're on!' her friends yelled.

Chapter
NINE

Storm marched back and forth, proudly
high-stepping round the gym. His tiny
red top hat leaned at a jaunty angle,
covering one ear. A sparkling red jacket
with shiny gold epaulettes and
matching buttons reached halfway
down his body.

Tracy wore her dress uniform of a
pleated skirt and a smart red jacket,

trimmed with gold braid. A red plumed
top hat and knee-length gold boots
completed her outfit.

The Limelight Majorettes were having
a full dress rehearsal. There was one day
left before the town parade. Tracy and
Helena, and the other members of the
B team, stood watching everyone
marching and twirling batons.

'Way to go, Kirsten! Storm's doing
great!' Tracy called out encouragingly,
clapping in time to the music. Although
she was trying to smile and look happy,

there was a wistful expression on her
face.

Kirsten knew her friend must be
longing to take part. She noticed that
Molly looked thoughtful. When
everyone stopped for a break, Kirsten
saw the trainer take Tracy aside and
have a word with her.

'I think Molly might be going to give
Tracy a second chance!' she whispered
to Storm.

Storm wagged his tail. 'I think so too.'

'Yay!' Tracy suddenly cheered and
punched the air before hurtling towards
the changing rooms. 'I'm in the A team,'
she sang out.

Everyone clapped, including Helena.
Kirsten had a big grin on her face.
She picked Storm up and whirled

around with him in a little dance of happiness.

Storm's tail twirled madly and he yapped with delight.

A few minutes later, Tracy reappeared, resplendent in full dress uniform, and proudly took her place in the ranks next to Kirsten.

'Up the LMs,' Helena shrieked, jumping up and down. 'Watch out, Kirsten. Watch out, Tracy. I'll be marching beside you next year.'

Kirsten looked towards her and smiled, her eyes glowing. 'I really hope so!' she called out.

The day of the parade dawned bright and clear.

Kirsten woke early. Two uniforms

were hanging from a hook on her bedroom door. She leapt out of bed, too excited to go back to sleep.

'Come on, Storm. We might as well start getting ready.'

Kirsten washed quickly and dragged a brush through her hair and then decided to give Storm a brush. He gave

her a pained doggy grin and managed
to put up with it for about half a
minute before he started play-growling
and trying to bite the brush.

Kirsten giggled. 'I get the message!'

Ten minutes later, she and Storm
stood side by side, looking in her
wardrobe mirror. 'Don't we look smart?'
Kirsten said admiringly.

She was too excited to eat breakfast
and only managed a mouthful of toast.
Her mum drove the short distance into
town. As Kirsten, Storm and her
parents emerged from the car park,
Kirsten saw Molly and the others at
the meeting point on the market
square.

'See you later,' she said to her mum
and dad, hurrying towards the LMs.

Tracy was already there and Helena was just arriving with her parents. She waved to Kirsten and Storm. 'Good luck. Knock 'em dead!' she cried.

Kirsten took a deep breath. 'This is it. Ready?' she whispered to Storm.

Storm nodded, holding his head high.

The Limelight Majorettes took their positions. The brass band began to play.

Sunlight glinted off the polished buttons and musical instruments.

Kirsten, Storm, Tracy and the rest of the majorettes moved forward.

The crowds cheered as the parade progressed through the streets. Coloured bunting fluttered from the stalls and smells of candyfloss and burgers filled the air. Entertainers juggled clubs, and acrobats tumbled through the air.

Kirsten twirled her baton, high-stepping in perfect time to the cheerful beat. Beside her, Storm's jaunty red hat nodded as he marched at heel.

The colourful parade moved through the streets. It seemed like no time at all to Kirsten before the majorettes and the band came to a halt. The lady mayor, wearing her gold chain over a smart blue suit, cut the ribbon and declared the new arcade open.

'Well done, everyone,' Molly said, beaming at her troupe. 'And well done, Storm. You're a perfect mascot. I suggest you all relax now and enjoy the entertainment.'

The delicious smells of food had made Kirsten hungry. She decided to buy a burger and share it with Storm.

But as she went to speak to him, he suddenly whimpered and tore away through the crowd.

Kirsten didn't hesitate. She ran after him and just glimpsed him dashing into a delivery bay at the rear of a shop. She whipped round at the familiar sound of growling and saw two large dogs some distance away. They were sniffing around under some parked vans.

A cold shiver ran down Kirsten's back as she saw their pale eyes and long sharp teeth.

Storm was in terrible danger.

Kirsten rushed into the delivery bay and slipped down between two parked lorries. Suddenly, there was a dazzling flash of bright gold light and sparks sprayed in all directions.

Kirsten saw Storm, a tiny helpless
puppy no longer, but a magnificent
young silver-grey wolf. His thick neck-
ruff looked as if it had been sprinkled
with a thousand tiny gold diamonds. An
older wolf with a gentle face stood
beside Storm.

And then Kirsten knew that her
friend was leaving. Her throat tightened

with tears, but she knew she would
have to be strong for Storm's sake.

'Quick, Storm. Your enemies are near.
Save yourself,' she urged.

Storm's big midnight-blue eyes
softened with affection. 'You have been
a true friend, Kirsten. Be of good heart.'

She rushed forward and threw her
arms round Storm's muscular neck. 'I'm
really going to miss you,' she sobbed,
her voice breaking.

Storm allowed her to hug him. He
held up one huge silvery paw as a final
burst of bright gold light filled the
delivery bay and sparks crackled down
around Kirsten and went out as they hit
the floor.

The two wolves faded and were gone.
On the floor by Kirsten's feet lay

something red and gold. Storm's tiny mascot uniform. A deep sadness swept through her, only made better by the relief at knowing that Storm was safe. She would never forget her wonderful friend and would always treasure the memories of their time together.

Kirsten heard a final fierce growl from behind her and then there was silence. She whirled round just in time to see two normal-looking dogs slinking away.

'Kirsten?' called a voice. Helena stood at the entrance to the delivery bay. She was holding a tiny puppy with shaggy light-brown fur. 'I just found Storm running around outside. I don't know how he got out of his uniform,' she said.

Kirsten did a double take. 'But that's not St–' Kirsten stopped as the strangest feeling came over her.

An image of Storm's mischievous face popped into her mind and then a knowing smile crept over Kirsten's face.

She gazed at the tiny puppy that looked just like Storm in almost every way. Only she would ever know that this wasn't Storm.

As the tiny lost puppy looked at her with frightened brownish-blue eyes, Kirsten knew exactly what she had to do. '*Storm*. Fancy running off like that,' she pretended to scold as she took the tiny puppy from Helena. 'I'll have to take really good care of you from now on!'

Win a Magic Puppy goody bag!

The evil wolf Shadow has ripped out part of Storm's letter from his mother and hidden the words so that magic puppy Storm can't find them.

Storm needs your help!

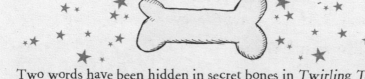

Two words have been hidden in secret bones in *Twirling Tails* and *School of Mischief*. Find the hidden words and put them together to complete the message from Storm's mother. Send it in to us and each month we will put every correct message in a draw and pick out one lucky winner, who will receive a Magic Puppy gift – definitely worth barking about!

Send the hidden message, your name and address on a postcard to:
Magic Puppy Competition
Puffin Books
80 Strand
London WC2R 0RL
Good luck!

Coming Soon

Magic Puppy

Start the new year with a sprinkling of magic...

Classroom Princess   *Friendship Forever*

puffin.co.uk